SEA WOLF

Rayne

Rayner, S.
Sea Wolf.

For Ross

ORCHARD BOOKS
338 Euston Road, London NW1 3BH
Orchard Books Australia
Level 17/207 Kent Street, Sydney, NSW 2000

First published in 2010
First paperback publication in 2011

ISBN 978 1 40830 261 3 (hardback)
ISBN 978 1 40830 269 9 (paperback)

Text and illustrations © Shoo Rayner 2010

A CIP catalogue record for this book is available
from the British Library.

1 3 5 7 9 10 8 6 4 2 (hardback)
1 3 5 7 9 10 8 6 4 2 (paperback)

Printed in Great Britain

Orchard Books is a division of Hachette Children's Books,
an Hachette UK company.

SEA WOLF

SHOO RAYNER

ORCHARD BOOKS

CHAPTER ONE

Axel Storm pulled hard on the tiller. The boat lurched and tilted. He ducked as the boom swung violently above his head. That was one lesson he had learnt well: "*Keep your head down!*"

Axel tightened the ropes, trimmed the sails and set a course for the new wind speed and direction.

"Congratulations," said an electronic voice. "You have completed the advanced sailing course. Press enter to print your certificate."

Axel was sailing the Sail Master Five, the most sophisticated and expensive land-based sailing machine in the world. Dad had bought it to keep him amused. Axel was now a master on dry land, but he had still never sailed on water!

"Can't I go sailing for real?" Axel sighed, as the fan motors switched off and the Sail Master boat came to a rest.

His mum adjusted her sun lounger to make sure she got an even tan. She looked over the top of her sunglasses and smiled. "Not while we're staying here, dear."

"The place is swarming with press photographers," Dad called from the hot tub.

Axel's mum and dad were rock stars. Their band, Stormy Skies, had recorded twenty-two platinum-selling hits in eighty-three different countries around the world. They spent half their lives travelling, performing concerts and meeting their millions of fans.

The Storms were rich – really, really rich. They were staying in their seaside mansion in Dolphin Bay.

In a few days they were going to join the luxury cruise liner, the *Queen of the Sea,* where they were giving a concert for a special celebrity cruise.

All the most famous and important people in the world were going on the cruise, so newspaper photographers and television reporters were everywhere.

"I bet Archie Flash, the photographer from *Celebrity Gossip Magazine*, is waiting on the beach right now," Mum said. "He'll do anything to get a picture of Axel."

"We want you to grow up like a normal boy," said Dad. "You can't be normal if your picture is in the papers all the time."

"You'll be nice and safe tomorrow," said Mum. "You're staying at Celebrity Kids' Club while we're on the cruise."

"Oh, *what*?" Axel wailed. "Don't make me go to Celebrity Kids' Club! You know I *hate* it. The Prime Minister's daughter was there last time. She thought she was in charge and kept making up rules until we weren't allowed to do *anything* at all!"

"It's been arranged," Dad said firmly. "Why don't you go for a last ride on the Surf Master Seven in the back yard?"

The Surf Master Seven was the most sophisticated and expensive land-based surfing machine in the world. Millions of gallons of seawater were pumped from the sea through a huge pipe, making every kind of wave you can imagine. It was a safe way to learn how to surf – no rocks, no dangerous currents and best of all – no sharks!

Axel stood up on his board as the machine put him through his paces. He raced down massive waves and swooped through tunnels of rolling breakers. As Axel came to the bottom of the steepest, fastest wave in the training mode, he pulled the toggle around his neck to switch off the Surf Master Seven.

He was bored. He'd done it all before
and he'd already got his platinum
certificate three times. He wished he
could surf for real.

The real seaside was just over the
other side of their security fence. The
sea was calling to him, offering real
adventure. But Mum and Dad wouldn't
let him go.

"Hey! What's that?" Axel noticed something floating in the Surf Master Seven surf pool. He leant in and pulled it out of the frothy bubbles.

"It's a message in a bottle," he laughed. "It must have got pumped up from the sea!"

Axel ran inside to look at the bottle more closely. "Hey! The message has my name on it! I wonder what it says?"

Dad helped Axel remove the cork. They shook the message out onto the table.

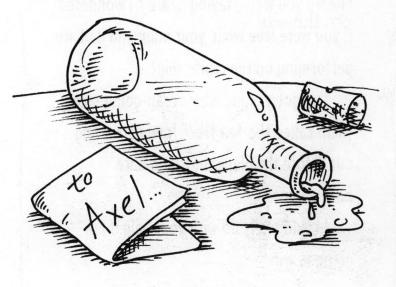

"It's from your Uncle Nelson!" Dad exclaimed. "I wonder what he wants?"

Axel read the message out loud.

Sea Wolf, Dolphin Bay.

Dear Axel,

I heard you were staying nearby. I wondered if you were free while your mum and dad are performing on the cruise ship?

I've got a brand-new ocean-going racing yacht called the *Sea Wolf*. It needs testing out before the Elephant Island Race next week.

I could really do with your help if I'm going to win.

Lots of love,
Uncle Nelson

"You are *not* going to race a yacht with Uncle Nelson!" said Mum. "*He* might be crazy enough to sail off round the world single-handedly, but you don't have any experience at sea."

"It's not a race," Axel pointed out. "He says the boat just needs testing out to make sure she works properly."

"But you're booked into Celebrity Kids' Club," said Dad.

Axel smiled. He knew how to get round his parents. "But this is a fantastic chance to put my sailing skills to real use," he said. "Otherwise *I've* wasted my time learning and *you've* wasted your money buying me the Sail Master Five training machine!"

Dad was stumped. He couldn't think of an answer to that!

"Oh, OK… But NO racing!" Dad ordered.

Axel grinned and saluted. "Aye, aye, Cap'n!"

CHAPTER TWO

Mum and Dad were still worried about
photographers, so they decided to take
Axel to Uncle Nelson in secret. They
hired a fishing boat for the day and
disguised themselves as local fishermen.

"Ahoy, there!" Uncle Nelson called,
as Dad cut the fishing boat's engines
and drifted alongside the *Sea Wolf*.

The *Sea Wolf* was magnificent.
She had twin hulls which were painted
electric blue, and a mast that soared
high into the sky like a missile. The
rigging clanked in the fresh breeze.

"Nelson!" Dad shouted as he leapt aboard.

"Thrust!" Nelson yelled, hugging his brother.

Uncle Nelson wore a sailing cap and had a big white beard.

"Axel!" He laughed and ruffled Axel's hair as he helped him on board. "My word, you've grown since I last saw you."

Axel smiled politely. Why did grown-ups always say that?

"Make sure you look after Axel,"
Mum said sternly. "He's not allowed
to go with you on the Elephant Island
Race. And keep him away from press
photographers!"

Uncle Nelson spread his arms wide.
"We won't get any photographers out
here," he laughed. "Not in the wild,
empty ocean!"

Mum and Dad climbed back into the fishing boat and chugged off to meet the *Queen of the Sea* for their cruise.

"We love you, Axel!" they called, leaning over the stern. "Make sure you wear your life jacket at all times. See you when the cruise is over!"

Axel watched them disappear over the horizon. He couldn't wait for his adventure to begin!

"Right, me lad," said Uncle Nelson. "Have you done any sailing before?"

"I've got a Sail Master Five advanced sailing course certificate!" Axel said proudly. "And I've got three platinum certificates on the Surf Master Seven!"

"Marvellous!" beamed Uncle Nelson. "But you might find sailing on real water is a little bit different!"

Uncle Nelson gave Axel a tour of the *Sea Wolf.*

First, he showed Axel how to use a
power winch to tighten the ropes that
controlled the sails.

Then he showed him where the
sails were stowed and how to work the
automatic tiller.

"The boat is controlled by satellite,"
Uncle Nelson explained. "We could go
to sleep for three days and the *Sea Wolf*
would keep sailing on the right course –
as long as we don't set it to sail into any
rocks!" he laughed.

Next, Uncle Nelson pressed a button. "This pulls up the anchor." A motor whirred somewhere below them and Axel heard the anchor chain being wound into the boat.

"And *this* is the boom," Uncle Nelson said in a serious voice.

"When we change direction, the boom swings across the deck," he continued. "It can knock you out, knock your block off, or knock you overboard, so—"

"Keep your head down!" Axel interrupted. "I learnt that lesson the hard way!" He rubbed his head, remembering when the boom of the Sail Master Five had nearly knocked him out. After having three stitches in his head, he would never let that happen again.

Uncle Nelson looked at his watch and scanned the horizon. Axel noticed that several other large sailing boats had appeared close by.

Suddenly there was a loud bang, and a green flare shot up into the sky.

"Hoist the mainsail! We're off!" Uncle Nelson roared.

"What? But I thought the race wasn't till next week! And…Mum said we weren't allowed to race," Axel said nervously.

Uncle Nelson smiled and raised an eyebrow. "We're just going out a hundred miles or so, round Elephant Island and then home again."

Uncle Nelson pointed out the route on a map.

"The other boats will be in the Elephant Island Race next week, too. We thought we'd have a little test run to make sure all the boats are ready. So we're not exactly racing…it's more like *the last one back is the loser*! Are you with me?"

Axel looked confused. "But…" he began. Then a broad grin spread slowly across his face. "What are my orders, Captain?"

CHAPTER THREE

The *Sea Wolf* shot into the lead. Even
though it wasn't strictly a race, Uncle
Nelson was an experienced ocean sailor
and he didn't like being behind!

"Why is the place we're heading for
called Elephant Island?" Axel yelled
over the wind.

Uncle Nelson laughed. "You'll see
when we get there!"

Axel sat in the cockpit as the *Sea Wolf* ripped through the water. Now that they were far out into the ocean, the waves were growing wilder and the wind was blowing harder.

Uncle Nelson tapped his barometer. "That's strange," he muttered. "The weather forecast said it was set fair all day. Where did that storm come from?"

Axel peered into the distance. Huge, dark clouds were rolling towards them. The sea was changing colour to a deathly shade of gunmetal grey.

Soon the enormous silhouette of Elephant Island loomed out of the towering waves. It was alive with birds that clung to the cliffs and wheeled and dived in the air around them. On one side of the island, an arch of rock swooped out into the sea.

"It looks like an elephant's trunk!" Axel said. Now the name of the island made sense.

Axel looked behind him to see if they
were still in the lead. But the other boats
were sailing in the opposite direction.

"They've turned back home!" Axel shouted into the wind.

"Aye!" Uncle Nelson said. "They're all a bunch of lily-livered landlubbers! We'll go round the island then head back to port. The Storm family have never been put off by a little bad weather!"

Rain lashed Axel's face as he followed his uncle's orders, tightening ropes and trimming the sails so the wind didn't capsize the *Sea Wolf*.

Seabirds pitched and screamed around their heads. Sometimes the *Sea Wolf* seemed to fly through the air, taking off from the foaming crests of giant waves. Then she'd heave down into the water and be engulfed by clouds of spray crashing over her bows.

Axel was too busy to be scared. The Sail Master Five had taught him well, but he'd never experienced the roaring noise or the violent movement of an angry sea before.

Sailing close to the island, Axel felt hemmed in between its dark towering cliffs, and the even darker cliffs of the thunder clouds that looked set to smash down on them at any moment.

Rounding the island, the giant stone arch of the elephant's trunk came into view. Just beyond the arch, they saw a small sailing boat that was battling against the elements.

"Idiot!" Uncle Nelson yelled. "He's not one of ours. What's he doing this far out to sea?"

A man in the boat was holding a bright-yellow object. He waved at them and shouted. The wind carried his voice over the water. Axel thought he heard the man call his name.

Just as the other boat shifted in the wind, Axel realised who it was. Then both he and Uncle Nelson saw the boom swing across the deck towards the man.

"Keep your head down!" they screamed.

CHAPTER FOUR

A massive bolt of lightning lit up the sky. The boom lurched across the deck and crashed into the man. It tossed him into the waves like a rag doll.

"It's Archie Flash!" Axel yelled. "He must have been trying to get photographs of me."

Archie's head bobbed up to the surface. His life jacket kept him above the water, but how long could he survive out there in the raging ocean?

Suddenly, the waves parted in front
of them, revealing vicious, jagged
rocks below.

"Rocks ahead!" Axel yelled.

Their only escape was to try and sail
under the arch of the elephant's trunk!
Uncle Nelson swung the tiller round and
aimed for the narrow channel of water
beneath the rock.

Archie's boat was lifted high on a wave and hurled against the rocks. In an instant it smashed into a thousand splinters.

Something scraped and clanged horribly under the *Sea Wolf.* Then it seemed to Axel as though the sky was collapsing all around them. The tall mast crashed into the elephant's trunk.

It snapped in two, dislodging rocks and sending acres of sail tumbling down onto the decks of the *Sea Wolf* below.

"YOWWL!" Uncle Nelson was pinned down by sails and rigging. A large rock plunged on top of him.

"I think I've broken my leg," he wailed. "I can't move it!"

Axel took in the situation. They were at the mercy of the swirling current that was dragging the *Sea Wolf* through the archway. If he didn't do something fast they were all going to drown!

"Try the engines!" Uncle Nelson groaned. Axel pressed the starter button, but nothing happened.

"I think we lost the propellers on the rocks!" Axel said.

They were adrift, with no sails and no power. In the distance, Archie Flash called for help.

A massive wave was building behind them. All Axel's training on the Surf Master Seven came to him in an instant. He pulled hard on the tiller and faced the *Sea Wolf* down towards the bottom of the wave.

"Let's go surfing!" he whooped.

The wave grew higher and higher – and steeper and steeper. The *Sea Wolf* rode up the side of the towering wall of water. Then she began to slide down the steep face of the wave, racing fast to keep ahead of the breaking crest behind her.

Archie Flash was close by. This would be their only chance of saving him from certain death.

Axel tied a loop in a rope and hurled it across to Archie. "Hold on tight!" he bellowed.

Archie caught the rope and struggled to get the loop over his head.

Axel wound the rope twice round
a winch and began hauling Archie in.

Uncle Nelson laughed in amazement. "I don't believe it! He's taking photographs!"

Sure enough, Archie Flash had a bright-yellow, waterproof camera. He was taking pictures as Axel hauled him on board the *Sea Wolf*, saving him from a horrible death. Archie's strongest instinct was to take pictures of great stories, and this would be one of his best.

CHAPTER FIVE

Archie Flash flopped onto the deck like a beached whale. "Say cheese!" he chirped, taking another action shot of Axel.

"If you're not careful," Uncle Nelson growled irritably, "I'm going to stick that camera of yours somewhere very painful!"

"When Axel didn't arrive at Celebrity Kids' Club," Archie panted, "I knew he'd be off on one of his adventures, so I hired a sailing boat and came after him."

Archie had never trained on a Sail Master Five. In fact, Archie had never sailed before in his life. It was beginner's luck that the wind had blown him as far as it did.

The storm was fading, but the waves were still strong. The *Sea Wolf* rolled helplessly on the water.

Axel found a professional first-aid kit down below. He used a blow-up splint to protect Uncle Nelson's leg and gave him some painkillers.

Uncle Nelson gritted his teeth. "You'll have to climb the mast and clear away the damage," he told Axel.

Inch by inch, Axel climbed high up into the rigging. He cut the ropes that held the useless, broken top of the mast.

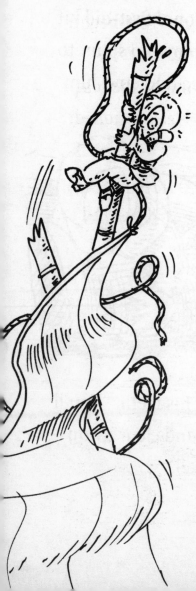

As he cut the last rope, the jagged, carbon-fibre masthead fell away and splashed into the sea far below him. Axel watched it sink slowly to the bottom of the ocean.

"Good lad!" Uncle Nelson called up to him. "Now lash that pulley to the top and thread a rope through it."

Soon, Axel had cut a sail down to size and hauled it up to the top of the broken mast. The fresh breeze puffed life into the sail and the *Sea Wolf* began her long, slow voyage home.

"I'm afraid we're going to be the last ones back to port," Uncle Nelson sighed.

"Better to be last than never get back at all!" Axel muttered, adjusting the tiller and bringing the *Sea Wolf* round into the wind.

"Say, cheese!" said Archie.

"*Keep your head down!*" Uncle
Nelson and Axel yelled as the boom
swung wildly across the deck.

CHAPTER SIX

"I don't believe it!" Dad wailed. "Axel is all over the papers and our concert hardly gets a mention!"

They were back at their mansion in Dolphin Bay. The papers and magazines were spread out on the table by the pool. They all showed Archie Flash's dramatic pictures and proclaimed Axel a hero.

The *Queen of the Sea* had also been forced back to port by the sudden storm. All the celebrities on board had been violently seasick and Mum and Dad's concert had to be abandoned halfway through when they ran out of buckets.

celebrities leaving the cruise yesterday

Mum scowled at Uncle Nelson, who was stretched out on a sun lounger close by. His plastered leg was raised on a mountain of cushions.

"It's all your fault!" she growled. "I told you not to go racing that stupid boat of yours with Axel."

"We weren't racing," Axel sighed. "It was *last one back is the loser.* That's a completely different thing."

"I don't know how you get yourself into these adventures," Mum sighed. "We only want you to have a normal life, you know."

Axel smiled and winked at Uncle Nelson. "I was just putting my sail and surf training into practice. I don't know *what* you're worried about!"

CELEBRITY GOSSIP MAGAZINE

YOUNG SAILOR OF THE YEAR and life-saving hero, Axel Storm, was captured in this thrilling set of pictures, rescuing our very own photographer, Archie Flash.

"I OWE HIM MY LIFE!"

said our ace photographer. "Without his quick thinking and extensive experience, we'd all be feeding the fishes by now."

Dave Masters, CEO of the Sail Master and Surf Master company, said, "Axel learnt his first-class sailing skills on our training machines, which are available exclusively through our website."

Axel was unavailable for comment.

His Uncle Nelson said, "That boy can really sail!"

By ace reporter, Archie Flash.

SHOO RAYNER

ALL PRICED AT £3.99

Orchard Books are available from all good bookshops,
or can be ordered from our website: www.orchardbooks.co.uk,
or telephone 01235 827702, or fax 01235 827703.